W9-COL-605

LOBSTER'S SECRET

SMITHSONIAN OCEANIC COLLECTION

Somerset County Library
Bridgewater, NJ 08807

To Alan, Mom, and Dad with love.
— K.H.

To H.R.W., R.L.W., K.R., and the boys,
who've always been there to protect me when I'm molting.
— J.W.

Book copyright © 1996 Trudy Management Corporation, 165 Water Street, Norwalk, CT 06854, and the Smithsonian Institution, Washington, DC 20560.

Soundprints is a division of Trudy Management Corporation, Norwalk, Connecticut.

All rights reserved. No part of this book may be reproduced or transmitted in any form or by any means whatsoever without prior written permission of the publisher.

Book Design: Shields & Partners, Westport, CT

First Edition
10 9 8 7 6 5 4 3 2 1
Printed in Singapore

Acknowledgements:
   Our very special thanks to Dr. Raymond Manning of the Department of Invertebrate Zoology at the Smithsonian's National Museum of Natural History for his curatorial review.

Library of Congress Cataloging-in-Publication Data

Hollenbeck, Kathleen M.

Lobster's secret / by Kathleen M. Hollenbeck ; illustrated by Jon Weiman.
        p.   cm.
Summary: Lobster emerges from his rocky hiding place off the Maine coast and prowls for dinner while watching for predators, a task made even more difficult after he molts.
        ISBN 1-56899-278-5
1. Lobsters — Juvenile fiction. [1. Lobsters — Fiction.]
I. Weiman, Jon, 1956-   ill. II. Title.
        PZ10.3.H716Lo 1996   95-45886
        [E] — dc20   CIP
                                                          AC

LOBSTER'S SECRET

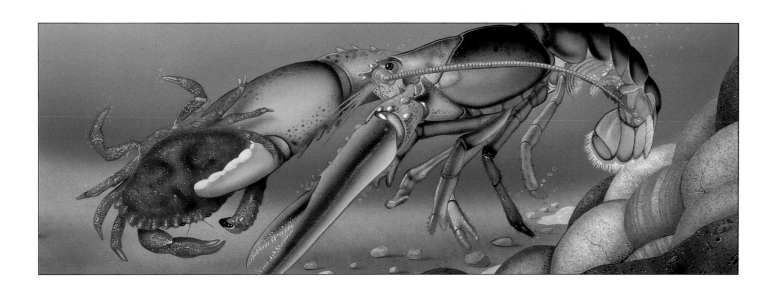

by Kathleen M. Hollenbeck   Illustrated by Jon Weiman

Soundprints
Where Children Discover Nature

The last rays of sun stretch across the rippling sea. A faded red buoy bobs lazily over the waves. Sea gulls call out overhead. Now and then they lunge down to catch fish for their supper. Some have already found rest on the rocky Maine shore.

Darkness falls on this late summer night. On the surface, the ocean seems peaceful and ready for rest. Yet, deep in the darkness below, creatures of the night begin to stir.

Crabs crawl out of hiding and scuttle across the ocean floor. Sea urchins scrape algae from rocks. Schools of codfish swim past in search of food.

Meanwhile, two slender pairs of antennae probe slowly, up and down, up and down. Tightly wedged in a hole between two rocks, Lobster waves his shortest antennae to learn if dinner — or danger — is near.

His antennae sense chemicals in the water coming from a tasty meal nearby. Hungry, Lobster crawls out of his hole.

Without warning, a codfish darts out of the blackness. Lobster pulls back into his den. He struggles, trying to fit his giant claws inside. As Lobster disappears, the codfish lunges.

Sharp teeth gnashing, the codfish
squeezes into Lobster's home. Lobster
presses against the rocks that form his den,
snapping his claws at the intruder and
ready for a fight. As the codfish closes in,
the rocks fall away behind Lobster. He
backs out into the open sea and away
from his enemy.

Still hungry, Lobster prowls for food.
Again his antennae sense food.

Antennae waving, Lobster follows the trail. On four pairs of legs, he walks across the ocean floor. His tiny eyes sway at the ends of tall stalks. They see only shadows.

Lobster feels mud, rocks, and plants with his claws, legs, and longest antennae. Tiny hairs line these body parts, touching and tasting Lobster's world.

On a bed of pebbles, Lobster finds his prey. A red rock crab raises its claws, perched and ready for battle. Lobster seizes the crab in his largest claw, the crusher. Boldly, the crab swings its own claws, trying to break free. But the crab's tiny claws are no match for Lobster's mighty ones. In one deadly swipe, Lobster tears off its claws with the sharp teeth of his own pincer. Then he carries the crab to his den.

After eating the crab, Lobster rests. He will need strength for the change that will soon take place. It is time for Lobster to molt. He will cast off his old shell and grow.

As Lobster molts, the back of his hard shell splits down the center. Lobster rolls onto his side and bends his body in half. Little by little, he pulls his body out of the cracked shell.

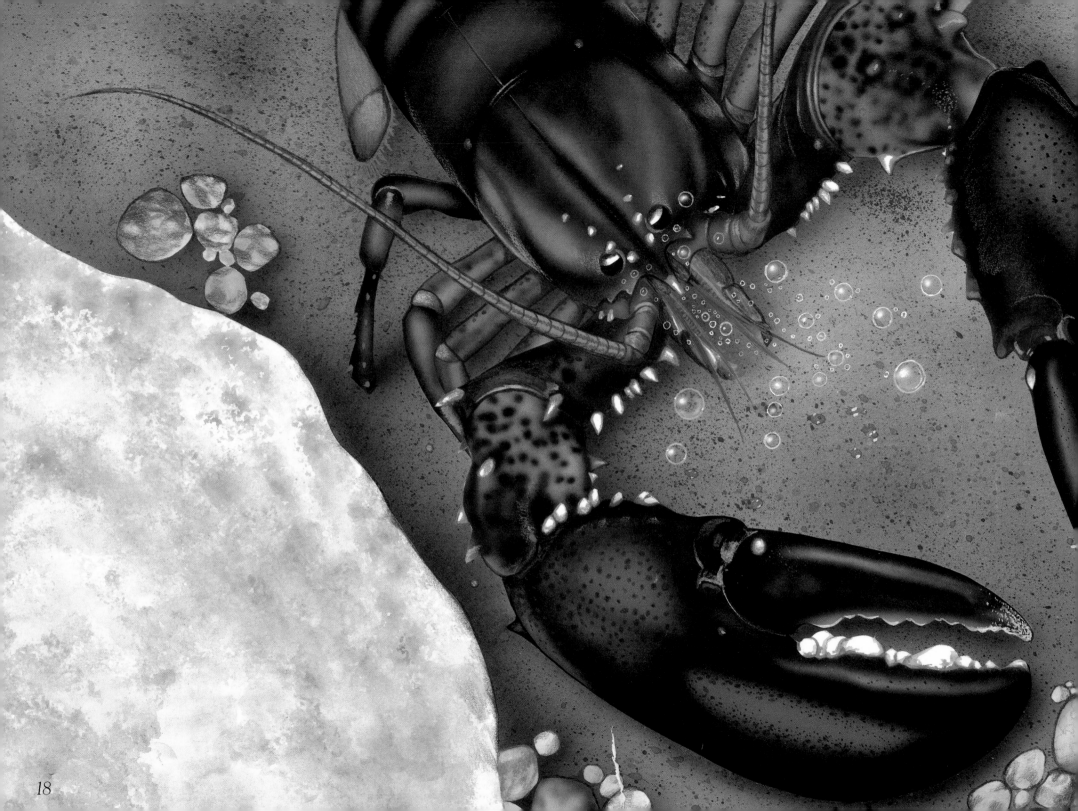

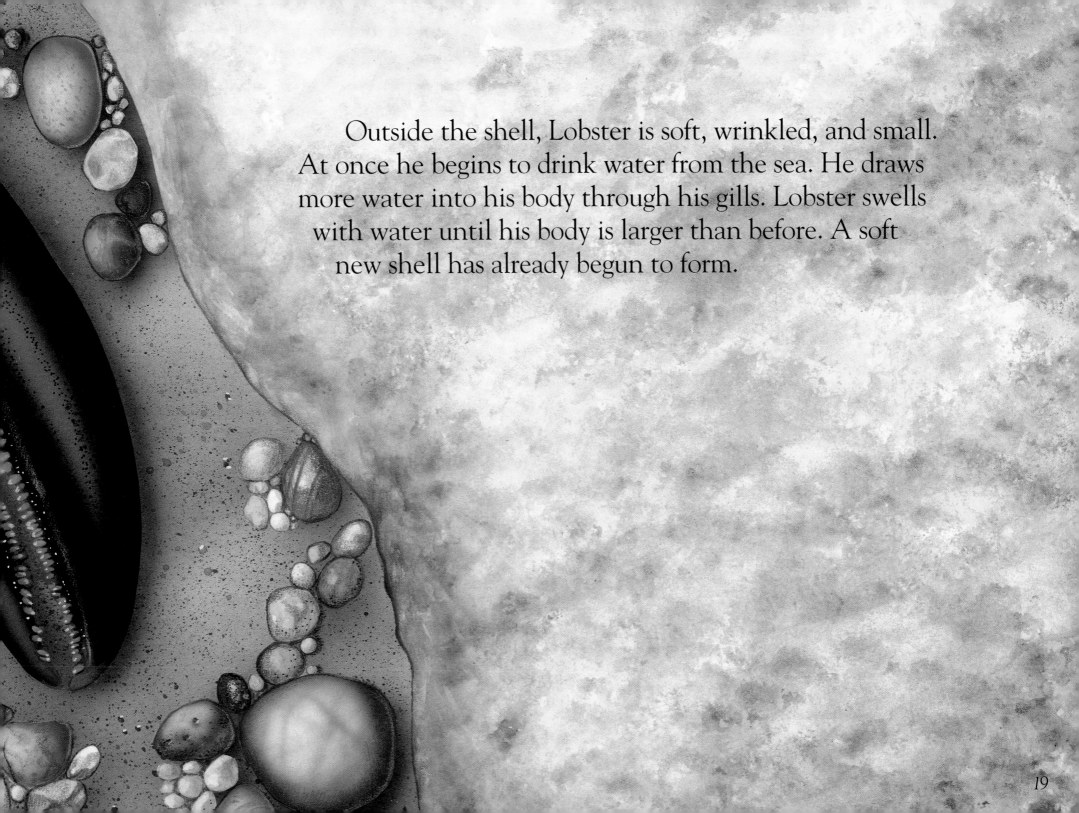

Outside the shell, Lobster is soft, wrinkled, and small. At once he begins to drink water from the sea. He draws more water into his body through his gills. Lobster swells with water until his body is larger than before. A soft new shell has already begun to form.

It will take weeks for Lobster's new shell to harden. Lobster helps by eating his old shell, rich with the minerals the new shell needs to grow strong.

Lobster rests in the safety of his den. He must hide from his enemies. His new shell is too soft to protect him.

After several days Lobster's shell is still soft, but now it looks hard and strong. Enemies will not know his secret. He ventures out of the den.

Hungry, Lobster walks across the ocean floor.
His antennae lead him to a large wooden cage, a
lobster trap. The food he senses is the bait inside.

Lobster climbs onto the
netting at one end of the trap.

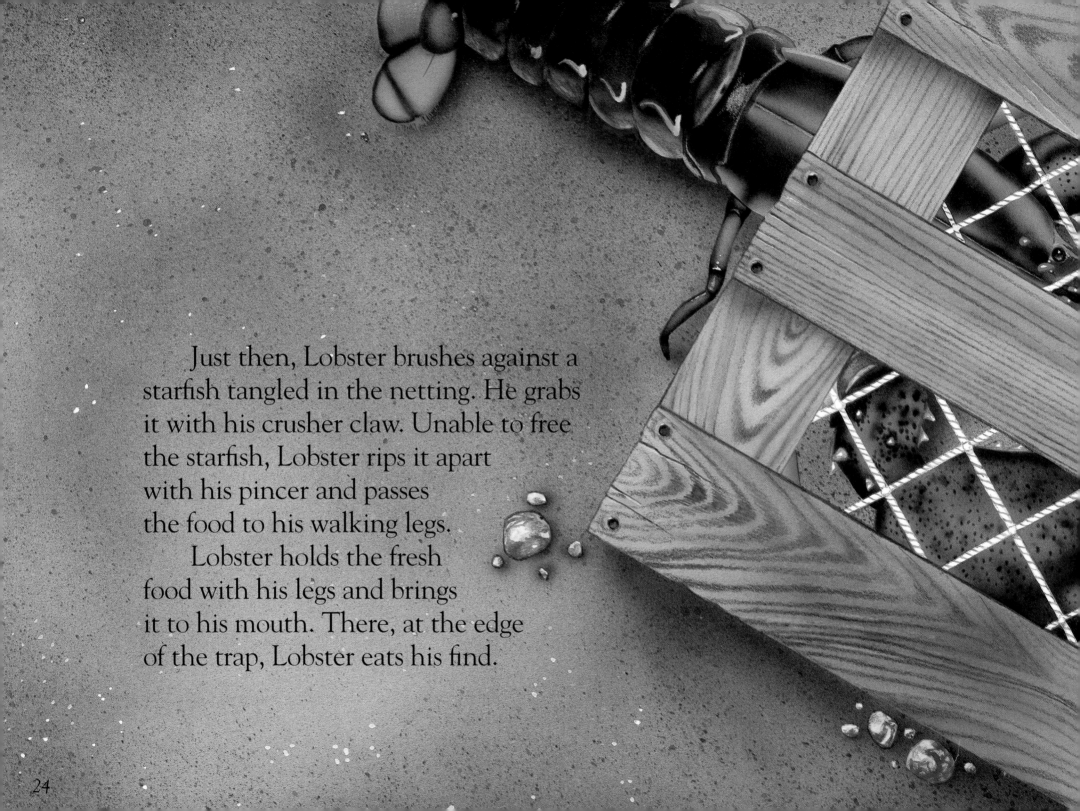

Just then, Lobster brushes against a
starfish tangled in the netting. He grabs
it with his crusher claw. Unable to free
the starfish, Lobster rips it apart
with his pincer and passes
the food to his walking legs.
Lobster holds the fresh
food with his legs and brings
it to his mouth. There, at the edge
of the trap, Lobster eats his find.

His antennae still sense the tasty bait, but Lobster is satisfied. He steps back onto the ocean floor. Suddenly, a sculpin lunges at him. Lobster jumps up, thrusts his antennae back over his head, and draws his walking legs in toward his body. Rapidly flexing his tail, he speeds backward through the water.

Lobster's eyes face backward as he races.
They help him find a hole among boulders
and he slips in easily. Snapping his claws fiercely,
Lobster warns the sculpin to stay away.

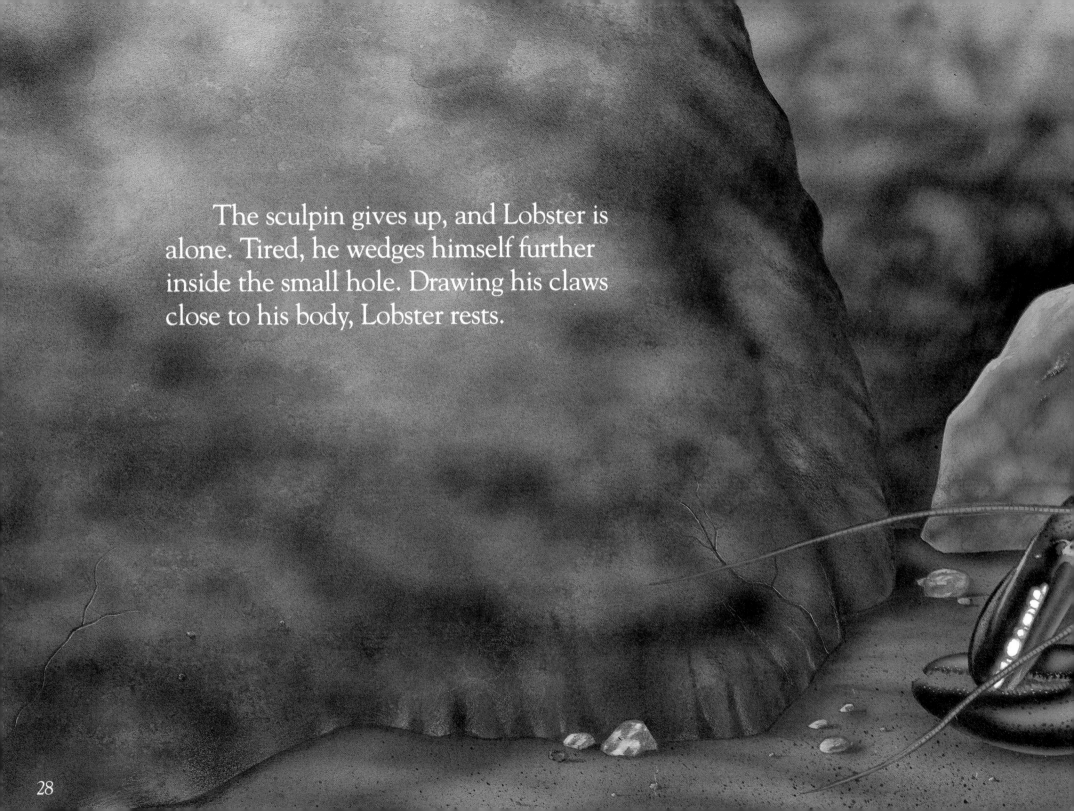

The sculpin gives up, and Lobster is
alone. Tired, he wedges himself further
inside the small hole. Drawing his claws
close to his body, Lobster rests.

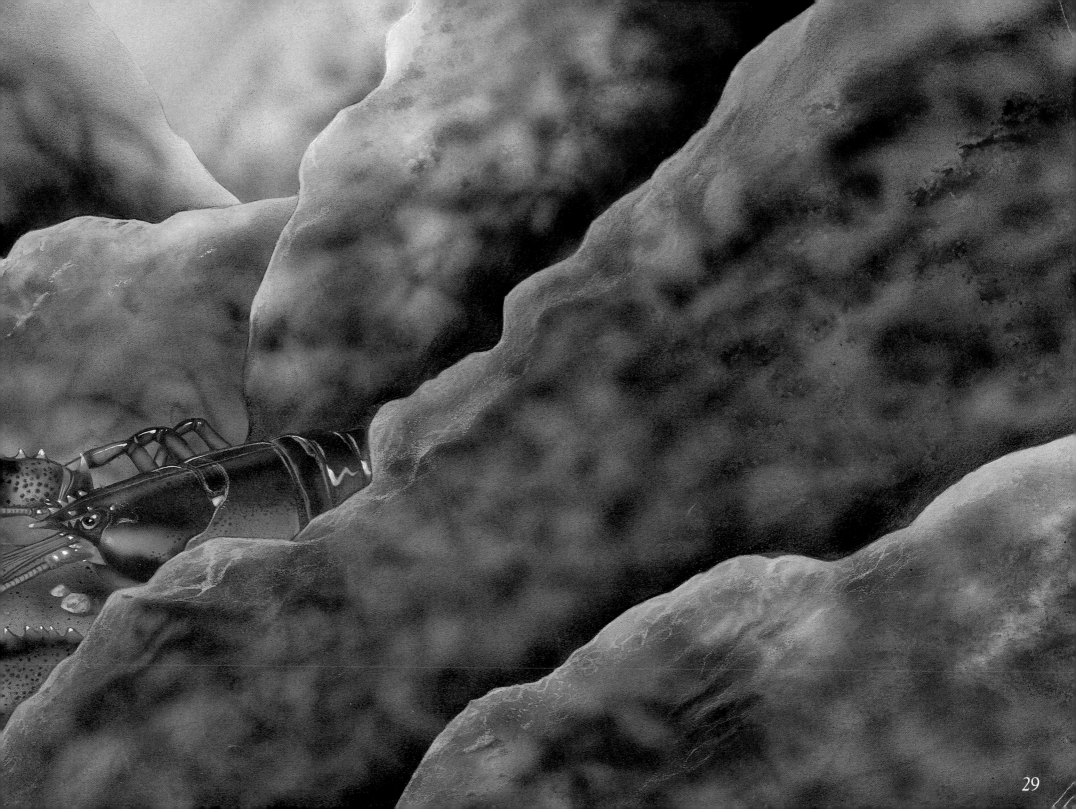

Soon night ends on the ocean floor. Crabs, codfish, and other night creatures rest in the shelter of rocks or plants.

Safe in his hideaway, Lobster waits for night to come again. In a few weeks Lobster's shell will be truly hard and strong. But for now his secret must be kept safe from his enemies until he is once again a fierce and sturdy creature of the sea.

About the American Lobster

The American Lobster can be found along the Atlantic coast of the United States and Canada. Its two enlarged front claws distinguish it from other kinds of lobster, which do not have them. The lobster is one of the largest crustaceans, measuring approximately 12 to 24 inches long and sometimes weighing up to thirty-five pounds.

Because its eyes do not see images the way we do, the lobster relies on sensory bristles, which cover its entire body, for touching, tasting, and navigating the ocean floor. The bristles on the lobster's antennae, for example, sense chemicals in the water, while shorter bristles on the inside of the walking legs and on some of the mouth parts allow the lobster to taste.

Lobsters grow by molting, or casting off their shells. During the first three years of life, lobsters can molt as many as nine times in a year. After this period, lobsters molt much less frequently... about once a year. Although the act of molting only takes 10 or 15 minutes, the new shell will not fully harden for 6-8 weeks. This leaves the newly-molted lobster vulnerable to its enemies and likely to spend much of its time in hiding.

Glossary

algae: aquatic plants that are green or red.

antennae: a pair of long narrow feelers on the head of an insect or crustacean.

bait: fish, crabs, or other food placed in a trap to lure animals.

buoy: a float used to mark a specific point in a body of water, such as the location of a lobster trap.

codfish: a stout fish, found in northern Atlantic coastal waters, that has a large mouth which it uses to prey on animals as big as lobsters.

lobster trap: a metal or wooden cage used to catch and hold lobsters.

molt: to shed an outer covering, such as a shell, in order to allow for new growth in its place.

pincer: the smaller of the lobster's two front claws, used for cutting and tearing.

sculpin: a fish commonly found in the shallows of the North Atlantic from Labrador to Cape Cod. The sculpin feeds mainly on lobsters, crabs, worms, and small fish.

sea urchin: a round marine animal with long sharp spines, found in shallow waters.

stalk: a movable stem that supports a lobster's eyes.

Points of Interest in this Book

pp. 6-7   six hole urchin, sea star, Atlantic rock crab, bamboo worm (tube-like, in foreground), purple sea urchins.

pp. 12-13   cushion star, sand dollar, common nutmeg (small shells), mouse cone (larger shell), sponge (light pink at right), red soft coral, tiger sharks.

pp. 30-31   red beard sponge (yellow, at left), finger sponge (bottom right).

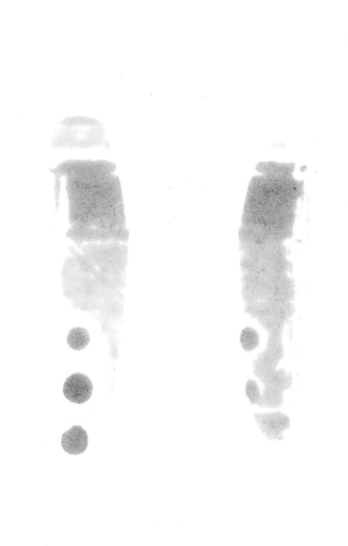

Picture HOLLENBECK
Hollenbeck, Kathleen M.
Lobster's secret

WATCHUNG PUBLIC LIBRARY
12 STIRLING ROAD
WATCHUNG, N. J. 07069

4/7/97